Dirty Bertie

WORMS!

For Christine ~ D R

To the lovely Hylands of Hyland Hall ~ A M

STRIPES PUBLISHING
An imprint of Magi Publications
1 The Coda Centre, 189 Munster Road,
London SW6 6AW

A paperback original
First published in Great Britain in 2006

Characters created by David Roberts
Text copyright © Alan MacDonald, 2006
Illustrations copyright © David Roberts, 2006

ISBN-10: 1-84715-004-7
ISBN-13: 978-1-84715-004-2

Printed and bound in Belgium by Proost

10 9 8 7 6 5 4 3

Dirty Bertie
WORMS!

DAVID ROBERTS WRITTEN BY ALAN MACDONALD

Stripes

Contents

CHAPTER 1

It was Monday morning and Bertie was eating his breakfast.

"Bertie, don't do that!" said his mum, looking up.

"Do what?" said Bertie.

"Let Whiffer lick your spoon. I saw you!"

"He's hungry!" said Bertie.

Dirty Bertie

"I don't care," sighed Mum. "It's dirty, Bertie."

Bertie inspected his spoon and gave it a lick. It looked clean enough to him.

Just then he heard the post thudding through the letterbox. He jumped down from the table and skidded into the hall. Bertie hardly ever got a letter, but it didn't stop him checking the post. He sorted through the bundle. Dad, Mum, Mum, Dad, boring, boring … wait!

A letter with his name written on it in large wonky letters!

To Bertie

Dirty Bertie

Bertie burst into the kitchen. "I got a letter!" He tore the envelope open. The decorations on the card could only mean one thing. A party!

Bertie loved birthday parties – he loved the games, the cake and the party bags. Last year he'd had a dog party and everyone had come as a dog. Bertie had been a bloodhound with Dracula fangs. He had wanted dog biscuits for tea but his mum had put her foot down.

Mum picked up the invitation. "Oh lovely, Bertie! Angela's invited you to her party."

"Angela?" said Bertie. The smile drained from his face. "Not Angela Angela?"

"Yes. Angela next door."

Dirty Bertie

"Bertie's little girlfriend!" teased his sister, Suzy.

Bertie grabbed the invitation and read the message inside.

Please come to my pink Birthday party on Friday! wear something pink! Love and kisses from Angela ×××

Bertie's mouth gaped open. His whole body drooped with disappointment. Angela Nicely lived next door and was almost six. She had straight blonde hair, rosy cheeks and large blue eyes. Worst of all she was in love with Bertie. She followed him round like a shadow.

Dirty Bertie

He didn't want to go to Angela's party, and he definitely didn't want to go to any party where you had to dress in pink. Bertie's favourite colour was brown. Mud was brown, fingernails were brown, poo was brown. Ribbons, bows and ballet shoes, they were pink.

"I don't have to go, do I?" asked Bertie.

"Nose, Bertie," said Mum.

Bertie removed a finger that had strayed up his nose.

"Angela's invited you," said Mum. "How would you feel if you invited Angela and she didn't come?"

"I'd feel glad," said Bertie, truthfully.

"It's a party, Bertie. You love parties," said Mum.

"And you love Angela!" taunted Suzy.

Dirty Bertie

Bertie ignored her. "It'll be terrible. They'll all want to play princesses. Couldn't you say I've got to go to the dentist?"

Mum gave him a look. "That would be a lie, wouldn't it, Bertie?"

"Mum! They'll all be girls," moaned Bertie. "I'll be the only boy!"

"I'm sure it'll be fun. Now, I'm late for work." She kissed him and hurried out. Bertie slumped into a chair.

A pink party with adoring Angela and her friends — could anything be worse?

CHAPTER 2

The next day Bertie overheard Mrs Nicely talking to his mum about the party. It was just as he feared. He was the only boy invited – along with six of Angela's friends. "Angela is so excited about Bertie coming," said Mrs Nicely. "I think it's so sweet she's invited her little boyfriend."

Dirty Bertie

Bertie was nearly sick. Boyfriend? Yuck!
He wasn't Angela's boyfriend! If his
friends ever heard about the party
they'd make fun of him for weeks. He
wasn't going and that was final. If his
mum wouldn't think of an excuse then
he'd have to invent one himself. When
it came to cunning plans, Bertie was a
master.

In his room he searched under the
bed for the shoebox where he kept his
top-secret possessions.

Dirty Bertie

He pulled out a notebook and began to write a list:

Brilliant excuses for not going to a party.

1. A crocodile bit my head off and I'm not talking to anyone.
2. I have got a rare disease called party-itis which brings me out in terrible spots.
3. I had baked beans for breakfast, lunch and supper. I think you know what that means.
4. I have lost my memory.

What party?

Dirty Bertie

Bertie read back through it. "Brilliant Excuse Number 4" would do the trick. Now all he had to do was talk to Angela and convince her. Then he would be off the hook. No stinky-pinky party for him.

Bertie's chance came on Wednesday lunchtime. He was eating lunch with his friends Darren and Eugene. They were flicking peas at the next table to see if they could land one down the back of Know-All Nick's jumper.

"Hello, Bertie!" said Angela, appearing from nowhere.

Bertie looked at her blankly. "Who are you?" he asked.

Angela giggled. "You are funny, Bertie! Did you get the invitation? You are coming to my party, aren't you?"

Bertie frowned. "Party? What party?"

"Silly! You know, my pink party!"

"PINK Party? Ha ha!" hooted Darren. "Bertie's going to a GIRL'S party!"

Bertie shot him a look. "Sorry, I don't remember any party," he told Angela. "I've lost my memory, you see."

"Gosh!" said Angela. "How?"

"That's just it, I can't remember. I must have got a bang on the head."

"Oh, poor Bertie!" cooed Angela.

Eugene and Darren exchanged glances. "Poor Bertie!" they mimicked.

Angela put her hand on Bertie's. Bertie drew it away quickly.

"Never mind," she said. "The party's at my house on Friday. We're having a bouncy castle."

"Have a nice time," said Bertie, loading more peas on to his spoon.

Angela stamped her foot.

"You've got to come, Bertie. Laura and Maisie are coming. I've told them you're my boyfriend."

Eugene gurgled and slipped off his chair. Bertie stared hard at Angela as if she looked faintly familiar. "Sorry? What did you say your name was?"

Angela gave a howl of rage and stormed off. Bertie heaved a sigh of relief. It had been a close call but he thought he'd got away with it.

Later that evening Mrs Nicely called to see his mum. Sensing trouble, Bertie hid in his room. But as soon as the front door closed, there was a shout from downstairs.

"BERTIE! Down here! Now!"

Bertie slunk downstairs.

"Right," said Mum. "What's this about losing your memory?"

Bertie stared at his feet. "Um ... yes. It just seems to keep um ... going."

"Really? So you don't remember Angela's invitation?"

Bertie knit his brows. "What invitation?" he asked.

Mum folded her arms. "That's a pity, because there's a film you wanted to see at the weekend. I expect you've forgotten that too?"

Bertie hadn't. "Pirates of Blood Island!" he blurted out. He'd been begging to see the film for weeks.

"Ah! So your memory *is* working," said Mum.

"I ... um ... remember some things. But other things I forget."

"Hmm," said Mum. "Well don't worry because I've marked the party on the

calendar to remind you." She pointed to
Friday the 8th – it was ringed in red.
"And Bertie…"

"Yes?"

"I will not forget."

Bertie slunk out of the kitchen.

He knew when he was beaten.

CHAPTER 3

Thursday sped by. Friday came. After
school Bertie played in his room with his
pet earthworm, Arthur. Bertie kept him
in a goldfish bowl filled with mud, leaves
and a plastic soldier for company. He
was trying to train Arthur to come
when he called him. "Arthur! Arthur!"
he coaxed.

"Bertie!" called Mum from downstairs.

"Just a minute!" shouted Bertie. He hid the bowl under the bed. His mum didn't exactly know about Arthur yet. A moment later she poked her head round the door.

"Come on, Bertie! You'll be late for the party."

"What party?"

"That's not going to work," said Mum.

"But … but … I haven't got a present," said Bertie, desperately.

Mum held up two boxes. "The doll or the face paints?" she said.

"Face paints," said Bertie, gloomily. He wasn't going to turn up holding a doll.

"Oh, and I bought you this to wear." Mum handed him a brand new T-shirt.

"Blech!" said Bertie. "It's pink. I can't wear that!"

"Don't be silly, Bertie, it's a pink party.
Now hurry up and get ready." She
disappeared, leaving him with the pink
horror.

Bertie retrieved Arthur from under
the bed. He held the T-shirt against him
and looked in the mirror.

"What do you think, Arthur?" he
asked. "Yucky or what?"

Dirty Bertie

Suddenly Bertie had the most brilliant brainwave. The invitation said to wear something pink. Well, worms were pink, weren't they? He could go to the party as an earthworm! All he needed was something pink and wormy to wear.

Bertie tiptoed into his parents' room. Strictly speaking he wasn't allowed in there, not since he'd used Mum's favourite perfume to make a stinkbomb.

Opening the wardrobe, he began to pull out armfuls of clothes. Nothing pink there. But then – bingo! – on top of the wardrobe he spotted something. Suzy's sleeping bag, the one she was taking to school camp. It was bright pink with a hood that fitted snugly over your head – perfect for an earthworm. All it needed was the finishing touch.

Dirty Bertie

Ten minutes later Bertie's mum found
him in the back garden.

"Oh, Bertie! No, Bertie!" she wailed.

"What?" said Bertie.

"You're filthy. Look at you!"

Bertie scrambled to his feet and
inspected his costume. He was
impressively dirty – but that was the
whole point of rolling in a flowerbed.

Dirty Bertie

"Earthworms are meant to be muddy," he explained. "They live underground."

"Bertie! I asked you to get ready for the party!"

"I am. It said to go in pink, so I am. I'm going as an earthworm."

Mum looked closer. "What is that?" she said. "It's not Suzy's sleeping bag?"

"It is!" beamed Bertie. "It's perfect!"

The sleeping bag was smeared with mud. It covered Bertie from head to toe with only his grimy face peeping out. Mum sat down heavily on the rockery.

"Bertie, you can't go like that."

"Why not?" said Bertie. "It's pink. I bet no one else'll be going as an earthworm."

"No," sighed Mum, wearily. "I doubt if they will."

CHAPTER 4

Angela's front door was festooned with
pink balloons. Mum walked up the path
with Bertie hopping after her like a giant
pink jumping bean and rang the
doorbell. Mrs Nicely came to the door.

"Hello!" she said and then, "Oh good
heavens!" as her eye fell on Bertie.

"I'm an earthworm," Bertie explained.

"How … ah … lovely, Bertie," said Mrs Nicely. "Do come in."

Bertie showered clods of earth on to the carpet as he bounced into the hall.

Most of Angela's friends had come as princesses and fairies. The front room was a sea of pink tutus.

"You're here, Bertie!" said Angela, running up to him. "I'm a fairy. Look, I've got wings!"

"I'm an earthworm," said Bertie. "I got you a present."

An arm emerged from the sleeping bag holding a scruffy package. Angela tore off the wrapping paper. "Thank you!" she trilled, dropping the face paints on top of her big pile of presents. Bertie gazed at them longingly.

"Let's play a game," said Mrs Nicely.

Dirty Bertie

"Who wants to play Musical Statues?"

"Me! Me!" chorused the fairies and princesses.

The music played and they all danced round the room.

"Bertie isn't dancing!" moaned Angela.

"Yes I am," said Bertie. "This is how earthworms dance!"

Bertie rolled over and over on the floor so that the dancing fairies had to jump over him. The music suddenly stopped.

Dirty Bertie

"Statues everybody! Statues!" cried Mrs Nicely. The fairies and princesses became wobbling statues. But Bertie, who was feeling a little hot and dizzy, hadn't been listening. He just kept rolling … straight into one of the fairies.

Laura wobbled and fell into Angela… Angela wobbled and fell on top of Maisie and Clare…

Soon all the statues had collapsed in a heap. Bertie rolled to a halt at Mrs Nicely's feet. "Did I win?" he asked.

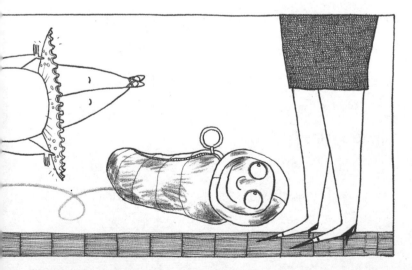

Dirty Bertie

Tea was pink. Pink biscuits, pink ice cream and a pink birthday cake in the shape of a heart. Bertie ate "worm-style" by licking things off his plate.

"Bertie, please don't slurp like that," sighed Mrs Nicely.

"Sorry," replied Bertie. "Worms can't help it. They don't know about manners."

Dirty Bertie

When tea was over Mrs Nicely surveyed the mess on the floor. Most of it had collected under Bertie's chair.

"Can we go on the bouncy castle now?" asked Bertie, tugging at her sleeve.

"In a minute, Bertie!" she said. "Angela, why don't you all go next door and play with your presents?"

While Angela's friends played with her Little Patty Pony set, Bertie eyed the face paints. Maybe he would just try one? He wriggled an arm out of his sleeping bag and selected a black face paint. He drew on his chin and looked in the mirror. Next he drew on his cheeks. Perhaps he would turn himself into a vampire or a zombie? Or better still…

He was so busy that he didn't notice the room had gone quiet.

Dirty Bertie

"Oh Bertie!" said Angela.

"Ah," said Bertie, "I was just … um … borrowing them."

"What have you done to your face?"

"I'm a slug," said Bertie.

"You said you were a worm."

"I was, but now I'm a slug. A big black, slimy slug."

He slithered on to the floor, making slimy, sluggy noises. Angela's friends shrieked with delight and ran to hide behind the curtains. Angela peeped out, her eyes shining. "Make me a slug too, Bertie," she pleaded.

Mrs Nicely was still tidying up when the doorbell rang. Thank goodness it was over for another year. She went to answer the door. Bertie's mum stood on the doorstep with three other parents.

"I do hope Bertie's behaved himself," she said.

"Oh yes," said Mrs Nicely. "He's such a … lively boy." She led them through to the back door. "They're all playing in the garden," she said. "Angela's had such a lovely time. They've all been good as…"

Mrs Nicely stopped in her tracks. Eight children were bouncing on the bouncy castle. But the princesses and fairies who had come to the party had vanished. In their place were ugly green monsters in filthy tutus who looked like they'd crawled from a swamp.

In the middle of them all was Bertie, bouncing and whooping.

Dirty Bertie

"Look, Mum!" sang Angela. "I'm a creepy caterpillar! Bertie did it!"

Mrs Nicely looked at Bertie's mum. The other parents looked at Bertie's mum. Bertie's mum looked at Bertie.

"What?" said Bertie.

Back in his room, Bertie was glad to be reunited with Arthur. Personally he couldn't see why everyone had made such a fuss. What was the point of giving someone face paints if they weren't allowed to use them?

"Anyway," he told Arthur with a smile. "I don't think they'll be inviting me next year."

He considered it. Really the party hadn't turned out so badly.

He felt in his pocket and brought out something pink and sticky.

"Look, Arthur!" he said. "I saved you some cake!"

CHAPTER 1

Bertie had no manners. His family all agreed. He lolled, he fidgeted and talked with his mouth full. He sniffed and slurped and burped and picked his nose.

"Bertie, use a hanky!"

"Take your elbows off the table!"

"Don't touch that, it's dirty, Bertie!" his parents moaned every day.

Dirty Bertie

Bertie didn't see the point. Animals didn't make all this fuss. Did pigs or dogs have manners? When Whiffer weed against a tree no one seemed to mind. Yet if Bertie had done that his mum would have fainted on the spot.

No, in Bertie's opinion manners were a waste of time. But that was before he heard about the prize.

It was the head teacher, Miss Skinner, who had announced the prize in assembly one morning.

"Does anyone know what tomorrow is?" she asked. Her gaze fell on Bertie who was crossing his eyes at Darren.

"Bertie!" she said.

"Uh … yes, Miss?"

Dirty Bertie

"Do you know what tomorrow is?"
Bertie thought. "Tuesday?" he said.

Miss Skinner gave him one of her
looks. "Tomorrow," she said, "is National
Courtesy Day. It's a day when we should
be especially polite, so I want us all to
think about our manners. We are lucky
to have Miss Prim from the library
coming to visit us, and she has agreed to
present a very special prize to the child
with the best manners."

"Huh! Special prize!" said Bertie to
Darren as they trooped back to the
classroom. "I bet it's some boring old
book about being polite."

"Actually it's not," said a reedy voice
behind them. It was Know-All Nick,
Bertie's worst enemy.

"How do you know?" asked Bertie.

Dirty Bertie

"Because I heard Miss Skinner tell Miss Boot," said Nick, looking pleased with himself. "She said the tickets had come this morning."

"Tickets for what?" asked Darren.

"Wouldn't you like to know!" sneered Nick (who would have liked to know himself).

"I bet it's football tickets!" said Darren.

"Or cinema tickets," said Donna.

"Or tickets for Mega Mayhem," said Bertie, his eyes lighting up. Mega Mayhem was the best theme park in the world and he'd been begging to go for months.

"It doesn't matter what it is," said Nick, smugly. "I'm bound to win. My mum says I've got beautiful manners."

"It's a pity your face is so ugly," muttered Bertie.

Bertie thought about the prize for the rest of the day. He was sure the tickets were for Mega Mayhem and he'd made up his mind to win them. Even if it meant he had to be polite for a whole day he didn't care. After all, how hard could it be?

CHAPTER 2

The next morning Bertie bounded out of bed. Today was National Courtesy Day – the day he was going to win the prize. On the landing he met his mum returning from the bathroom.

"Good morning, Mum," he said. "Isn't it a lovely morning?"

His mum gave him a suspicious look.

Dirty Bertie

"What have you done, Bertie?"

"I haven't done anything," said Bertie. "I was just being polite."

Downstairs Dad and Suzy were eating breakfast.

"Good morning!" Bertie greeted them cheerfully, as he sat down.

He poured Frostie Flakes into his bowl and cleared his throat. "Ahem. Would you pass the milk please, Suzy?"

Suzy stared at him. "Why are you talking in that funny way?"

"It's not a funny way, thank you. It's called being polite."

Bertie poured milk into his bowl without spilling a drop and sucked his Frostie Flakes so as not to make a noise. Even when he dropped his spoon he was careful to wipe it on his jumper before putting it in his mouth.

"I might be getting a prize today," he announced.

Dad looked up. "Mmm? What kind of prize?"

"For being polite," said Bertie. "It's National Courtesy Day and they're giving a prize for being polite."

"You? Polite? HA!" snorted Suzy.

Bertie sniffed. "I'm more polite than you, fat-face."

"Nose, Bertie," said Dad. "Where's your hanky?"

Bertie pulled a grubby hanky from his pocket and wiped his nose. Something fell out and plopped into the sugar bowl.

Dirty Bertie

"Eugghh!" shrieked Suzy. "What's that?"

"It's only Buzz. He won't hurt you," said Bertie, picking out the large bluebottle.

"Bertie! It's a dead fly!" said Dad.

Dirty Bertie

"I know," replied Bertie. "Don't worry, I'm going to bury him."

Bertie had found Buzz lying on his window sill. He had decided to bury him under the apple tree. He blew off the sugar that was stuck to his wings.

"Put it away!" said Dad. "It's filthy!"

Bertie sighed and wrapped Buzz inside his hanky. He would bury him after school. That was the trouble he thought, you did your best to be polite and all you got was people shouting at you.

CHAPTER 3

Miss Prim stood at the front of the class. She was tall and thin. Her glasses hung round her neck on a cord. Bertie thought she must be a hundred at least. He'd seen Miss Prim at the library where she stood behind a desk and stamped people's books. He hoped she didn't remember him. Last time he'd been to the library Whiffer had done something in the story corner and they'd had to leave quickly.

"This is Miss Prim," said Miss Boot. "I hope we're all going to show her how well-mannered we can be." She ran her eye over her class, who were all sitting up straight and paying attention. It was marvellous the effect a prize could have. Even Bertie wasn't lolling in his seat or pushing a pencil up his nose.

Miss Prim talked to the class about the importance of good manners. Bertie tried to listen but his mind kept drifting off. He was imagining whizzing down the Slide of Doom at Mega Mayhem.

"Now," said Miss Boot. "Who would like to show our visitor around the school? Let's have two volunteers."

Dirty Bertie

Bertie's hand shot in the air. This was his chance to show Miss Prim how polite he could be. Unfortunately everyone else in his class had the same idea. Thirty children strained out of their seats waving their hands in the air. "Miss! Ooh, Miss! Please, Miss!"

Miss Boot pointed. "Nick. I'm sure you'll look after our visitor."

Bertie couldn't believe it. Not Know-All Nick – why did he always get picked? Just because he'd made Miss Boot a soppy card on her birthday. It wasn't fair – Bertie never got picked for anything.

Miss Boot hesitated. She needed someone else who was polite and reliable.

"Miss, ooh, Miss! Me, Miss!"

"What about that boy at the back who's sitting so quietly?" suggested Miss Prim.

"Oh," said Miss Boot. "Not Bertie?"

Bertie, who hadn't been listening, looked up. "Me?" he said.

Miss Prim walked down the corridor, admiring the paintings on the walls.

"That one's mine," said Nick, pointing to a bright picture of a sunset.

"And that one's mine," said Bertie, pointing to a splodgy mess of green. "It's an alien. And that's his dinner inside him."

"Ah," said Miss Prim. "How unusual. Don't we have a hanky, Bertie?"

"Oh yes. 'Scuse me," said Bertie. He pulled out his hanky and offered it to Miss Prim.

"No, I meant you. You need to wipe your nose!"

"Oh. Thanks," said Bertie. He wiped his nose on his sleeve and pocketed his hanky. He'd just remembered Buzz was wrapped inside and he didn't want him falling out.

Miss Prim sighed heavily. "Perhaps we could look in the next class," she said.

Nick started to walk ahead quickly. Bertie kept pace with him. There was a mad dash for the door and they both grabbed the handle at once.

"I was first!"

"I was!"

"I was!"

Miss Prim caught up with them. "Boys, boys! I hope we're not squabbling," she said.

"Oh no," smiled Nick. "I was just telling Bertie his shirt's hanging out."

Bertie looked behind him. Nick wrenched open the door, squashing Bertie behind it.

Dirty Bertie

"After you, Miss," said Nick. Miss Prim beamed at him.

"Thank you, Nicholas. It's nice to see someone remembers their manners."

CHAPTER 4

By lunchtime Bertie was exhausted.
Being polite was hard work, especially
with Know-All Nick trying to outdo him
the whole time. And now it looked as if
he was stuck with Miss Prim for lunch.

As they crossed the hall, Bertie could
hardly believe his eyes. No one in the
dinner queue was pushing and shoving.

Dirty Bertie

There was no running or fighting or firing peas across the room. Everyone was eating their lunch quietly and politely.

"Hello, Miss Prim!" called Donna, as they passed by.

Bertie gulped. Three of his teachers were waiting for them at a table laid with a white tablecloth and a vase of flowers.

"Do come and join us," said Miss Skinner. "Bertie will fetch your lunch."

"Careful you don't drop it, Bertie!" whispered Know-All Nick.

"Careful I don't drop it on you," muttered Bertie.

Bertie sat opposite Miss Prim and Know-All Nick and stared at the plate in front of him. Spaghetti — how was he meant to eat that without making a mess? He watched Miss Prim wind spaghetti round her fork and tried to copy her. The spaghetti fell off before it reached his mouth. Nick put a hand over his mouth and loudly sucked up a piece of spaghetti. "Shlooooooop!"

"Bertie!" he said. "Don't be so disgusting!"

The teachers all looked in Bertie's direction.

"But … it wasn't me!" gasped Bertie. "It was him!"

Miss Prim made a tutting noise. "Don't tell tales, Bertie, it isn't nice."

Bertie turned to glare at Nick. He would have liked to put spaghetti down his neck. He would have liked to pour a jug of water down his pants. But he wanted those tickets and Miss Prim was watching him like a hawk. As he lifted his fork to his mouth a hand jogged his elbow.

SPLAT! A splodge of sauce landed on the white tablecloth.

"Oh Bertie, you are messy!" jeered Nick. "Look what you've done!"

Miss Prim made another tutting noise.

"But it wasn't ME!" shouted Bertie.

Miss Boot glared.

Bertie ground his teeth. He would get that two-faced slimy sneak.

Nick was sent to fetch dessert.

Bertie's eyes lit up. Chocolate fudge cake – his favourite. He reached out to grab a piece.

"Manners, Bertie," Miss Prim reminded him. "We don't grab, we offer the plate to others."

Bertie reluctantly passed the cake round the table. Miss Skinner took a slice, so did Miss Boot and Mr Plumly. Bertie watched anxiously as the cake began to disappear.

"Oh dear," said Miss Prim, helping herself. "Only one piece left! Which of you is going to have it?"

Dirty Bertie

Bertie looked at Nick. Nick looked at Bertie. Both of them eyed the last slice of fudge cake. Then Nick did a surprising thing – he offered the plate to Bertie.

"You have it, Bertie," he said with a sickly smile. "I don't mind, really."

Bertie wasn't going to fall for that one. "That's okay, Nick, I want you to have it."

"Oh, well, if you insist," said Nick. "We don't want it going to waste." He snatched the last piece and took a large bite. "Thanks, Bertie."

Dirty Bertie

Bertie glared furiously. He'd been tricked! Well, that was it. No more manners, this was war. That fudge cake was his by right and he was going to get it back. Bertie reached into his pocket and brought out his hanky. Nick was too busy talking to Miss Prim to notice a hand dart across the table.

"Any second now," thought Bertie. "Five, four, three, two…"

Nick reached for the cake and raised it to his mouth. There was something black on top.

"ARGHHHHH! A fly!" screamed Nick, dropping the cake on the table.

"ARGGHHHH!" shrieked Miss Prim as Buzz landed in front of her.

"I'll get it!" cried Miss Skinner. She seized a spoon and attacked the bluebottle.

Dirty Bertie

SMACK! WHACK! THUMP! Plates and cups leaped in the air. Buzz hopped and jumped with each blow, showing surprising speed for a dead fly.

Miss Boot grabbed the water jug and emptied it over the table. SPLOOSH!

Buzz lay still in a puddle with his legs in the air.

"Is it dead?" asked Miss Skinner. She picked up the fly by one leg and examined it.

Dirty Bertie

The silence was broken by a loud burp.

Six pairs of eyes turned on Bertie. He had cake crumbs round his mouth and a satisfied smile on his face.

"Bertie!" said Miss Skinner.

"Um… Pardon me!" said Bertie, politely. He held out his hand. "Could I have my fly back, please?"

Later that afternoon Bertie crowded into the hall with everyone else. The moment had arrived for Miss Prim to announce the winner of the prize. Bertie knew he didn't stand a chance – not after all the trouble at lunchtime. At least he'd been able to rescue Buzz from the litter bin. In any case it had all been worth it to see the look on Know-All Nick's face when he'd come eye to eye with Buzz. Bertie didn't mind who won the prize – as long as it wasn't Nick.

"And the winner," said Miss Prim, "is Nicholas Payne."

Bertie groaned. Know-All Nick made his way to the front and shook Miss Prim's hand. Everyone craned their necks to see what his prize would be. Miss Prim handed him an envelope. "As you're always so polite I'm sure you're going to love this. It's two tickets for the Museum of Manners in London."

Nick turned white. His mouth gaped open but nothing came out.

Bertie leaned forward. "Manners, Nick," he said. "Aren't you going to say thank you?"

Dirty Bertie

CHAPTER 1

RUMBLE, RUMBLE! SCREECH! SNORT!
Something was making a noise outside
Bertie's window. He sat up in bed. It was
Saturday, Bertie's favourite day of the
week. Saturday was bin day. He pulled
back his curtains. Sure enough, there was
the dustcart at the far end of the road.
If he hurried he would be just in time.

Downstairs he found Mum making tea in the kitchen.

"Morning, Bertie…" She broke off and stared at him. "What on earth are you wearing?"

Bertie looked at his outfit. He had on his dad's painting overalls, a woolly hat and a muddy pair of wellingtons. True, the overalls were a bit big, but Bertie thought they were perfect for a bin man.

Dirty Bertie

"It's Saturday," he said. "I've got to help Ed with the bins."

"Oh Bertie, not today," sighed Mum.

"Why not?"

"It's the summer fair this morning. I don't want you getting filthy."

"That's why I'm wearing these!" said Bertie, flapping his long sleeves.

"Anyway," said Mum, "you're too late. I took the rubbish out last night."

"But I always do it!" cried Bertie.

"Sorry, I forgot. You can do it next time."

He stared after his mum as she disappeared upstairs with her tea. Whiffer looked up from a bone he was licking and blinked at him. "How could she forget?" asked Bertie. "I always take the rubbish out on Saturdays!"

Dirty Bertie

When he grew up Bertie had decided he wanted to be a bin man. He wanted to wear an orange jacket and big gloves and ride in a truck that snorted like a dragon. Most of all he wanted to work with mountains of messy, smelly, sticky rubbish. Bertie loved rubbish. He had piles of it under his bed. String, lolly sticks, rubber bands, sweet wrappers – it was amazing what people threw away!

He began to rummage in the drawers. The bin men would be here any minute. Finally he found what he was looking for – a large black bin bag. All he needed now was a few bits of rubbish to fill it. Bertie looked around.

In went a dishcloth, a bar of soap, a tin of cat food and a pile of letters from Bertie's school (no one ever read them anyway). In went his dad's slippers, some carrots (yuck!), a cauliflower (double yuck!) and his sister's pony magazine.

Rumble, rumble! The dustcart was coming. Bertie scooted into the hall dragging his bag behind him. Someone had left a pot of old flowers by the front door ready to throw out. Bertie scooped it into the bag with the rest.

Dirty Bertie

The wheelie bin stood on the pavement. Bertie climbed on to the front wall so he could reach to drop his bag in. He peered into the bin, sniffing the sweet smell of rotting vegetables.

In one corner he caught sight of something familiar. Wasn't that his chewing gum collection? Surely his mum hadn't thrown it out? He bent into the bin to try and rescue it. The jar was just out of reach of his fingertips. He'd have to… "ARGHHH!"

Bertie toppled in head first.

Dirty Bertie

His face was wedged against something soft and squashy. "Mmff! Help!"

"Hello, mate," said a voice. "Having a bit of trouble there?" Strong hands pulled him out and set him on his feet.

"Oh dear!" grinned Ed. "Your mum's going to be pleased."

Bertie inspected himself. He did seem to have got a bit messy. There was something sticky on his overalls that smelled like tomato ketchup. He brushed off some tea leaves and straightened his hat. A piece of potato peel fell off. He held up the rescued jam-jar to show Ed.

"I was looking for this. It's my chewing gum collection," he explained. "I'm doing an experiment to see what happens when it gets really old."

"And what does happen?" Ed asked.

"It goes hard and it tastes really disgusting," said Bertie. "Want to try a bit?"

"No thanks," smiled Ed. "I've got to get on. Want to give me a hand?"

"Yes please!" said Bertie. "I brought you an extra bag today."

Bertie presented him with the rubbish he'd collected. Ed dropped the bag in the wheelie bin and Bertie pulled it to the waiting truck. He watched fascinated as the truck opened its metal jaws and swallowed up the rubbish. Ed held out a gloved hand and Bertie shook it.

"Good work, mate," said Ed. "See you next week." He moved off down the road, whistling.

"See you!" called Bertie.

CHAPTER 2

Back in the house, Bertie whistled as he spooned dog food into Whiffer's bowl. He whistled as he took off his overalls and sat down to have some breakfast.

"Bertie, please!" said Dad.

"What?" said Bertie. "I'm only whistling."

"That isn't whistling. You sound like you've got a puncture."

Dirty Bertie

"Well I've got to practise," said Bertie. "How can I learn to whistle if you don't let me practise?"

Mum came into the kitchen looking flustered.

"Bertie, have you seen my flower arrangement? I left it by the front door this morning."

Bertie paused with his finger in the peanut butter. "By the door?"

"Yes, it's for the competition at the summer fair. I spent hours working on it and now it's disappeared. Are you sure you haven't seen it?"

"Me? Um … no."

"Are you all right? You look a bit pale."

"I'm fine," said Bertie, who suddenly wasn't feeling so well. He remembered the pot of old flowers by the front door. He remembered putting it in his rubbish bag. Uh oh – the dustcart must have eaten it. Now he thought about it his mum had been going on about the competition for weeks. First prize always went to Mrs Nicely next door, but this year Bertie's mum felt she stood a chance. Or she would have done… How was Bertie to know the flowers by the door were hers? They looked practically dead!

He got up from the table and sidled towards the door.

"Where are you going?" asked Mum. "You haven't finished your breakfast."

"I just need to do something."

"And what's this all over Dad's overalls?"

"Just ketchup. I had a bit of an accident."

"Bertie…!"

But Bertie was making for the door. If he was going to get those flowers back he would need to move fast.

CHAPTER 3

Bertie bent over the handlebars of his
bike, pedalling at top speed. Whiffer
scampered behind, trying to keep up.
Maybe he was too late already. Even if
he caught up with the dustcart, how
was he going to get the flowers back?
Ed had told him all the dustcarts took
their loads to an enormous dump.

Dirty Bertie

Perhaps Ed would let him hunt through the mountains of rubbish there? Bertie loved the idea of that. But at the end of the road there was no sign of either Ed or the truck. By now it might be miles away. He sped on towards the park and slammed on his brakes at the corner. There, parked a hundred metres away, was the dustcart.

"Hey!" called Bertie. "Hey, wait a minute!"

The truck was starting to pull away. It got up speed, turned a corner and vanished out of sight. Bertie looked down at Whiffer whose ears drooped in sympathy.

He was sunk. Mum would scream. Dad would shout. He would be sent to his room for a million years.

Dirty Bertie

"Bertie, is that you?" called Mum as he crept in through the front door.

"No," answered Bertie.

"I want a word with you. Now."

Bertie drooped into the kitchen where Mum, Dad and Suzy were waiting for him. He could tell by their faces that he'd been rumbled.

Dirty Bertie

"Where are my slippers?" said Dad.

"Where's my *Pony Weekly*?" asked Suzy.

"And what have you done with my flower arrangement?" demanded Mum.

"Me? Why do I always get the blame?" protested Bertie. "It's not my fault if people keep losing things!"

Mum folded her arms. "Look at me, Bertie. I want the truth. Did you touch those flowers?"

Bertie tried to look at his mum. "I might have um … given them to someone," he mumbled.

"I told you!" said Suzy.

"Who?" demanded Mum.

Bertie tried to think of an answer. He wanted to tell the truth but the truth was he'd given the flowers to a dustcart.

Dirty Bertie

By now they were probably buried
under six feet of cabbages and nappies.

"I gave them to … Gran!" he said with
sudden inspiration.

"Gran? What on earth for?"

"She likes flowers," said Bertie. "She
likes smelling them and stuff."

Mum looked unconvinced. "And when
did you do this?"

"This morning," said Bertie. "I saw
them by the front door and I thought I'd

take them to Gran to cheer her up."

His family stared at him. Bertie had never given flowers to anyone before. On the other hand, he had been known to do all sorts of weird things. Mum's expression softened a bit.

"Well it was a nice thought, Bertie, but I need those flowers back. They've got to be at the church hall by ten. I'll give Gran a ring."

She picked up the phone.

"No!" said Bertie, desperately. "I'll go round! It'll be quicker. She's probably finished smelling them by now."

Mum replaced the phone. "All right, but you'd better hurry. If I miss this competition you're in serious trouble."

Dirty Bertie

Bertie set off with Whiffer padding beside him. At the end of the road he sat down on a wall to think. Now what was he going to do? Bringing Gran into it had only made things worse. Now Mum expected him to come back with her stupid flower arrangement. He stared gloomily at Whiffer who was sniffing around the garden behind him. The house was empty and the front garden overgrown with tall weeds.

Suddenly Bertie had a brilliant idea. What was to stop him making his own

flower arrangement? It would be easy!
There were hundreds of flowers right
here that nobody wanted. All he had to
do was pick a handful, stick them in a
pot and enter it in the competition. If he
took it to the church hall himself, his
mum might never find out.

Half an hour later Bertie had put his
plan into operation. The new flower
arrangement had been safely delivered
to the hall. He hurried home to tell his
mum the good news.

CHAPTER 4

The summer fair was in full swing when Bertie and his family arrived. He trailed round the stalls with Whiffer on his lead. There were stalls selling plants and home-made jam but nothing to interest Bertie. For some reason, Whiffer kept whining and pulling him back to the table displaying the flower arrangements.

Dirty Bertie

Mrs Nicely was standing by the table, talking to Bertie's mum. "I don't know what I'd do if I won again," she was saying. "It would be too embarrassing."

"I can imagine," said Bertie's mum. "So which one is yours?"

"Oh, that little vase of tiger lilies," said Mrs Nicely, pointing to a towering display of yellow blooms. She lowered her voice and pointed. "Can you believe someone actually entered that ghastly mess?"

Dirty Bertie

Bertie stared at the "ghastly mess".
It was a cracked pot with dandelions,
grass and twigs sticking out in all
directions. In the middle was what
looked like a dog's bone.

"Actually," said Bertie, loudly, "I think
that's the best of them all."

Mum pulled him to one side. "Bertie,
where's my flower arrangement?
I thought you said you gave it in."

"Um … I did," said Bertie. Luckily, at that moment, he was interrupted by one of the judges.

"Can I have your attention? We're about to announce the results of the flower arranging competition," he boomed.

Second prize went to Mrs Nicely who tried hard not to look disappointed. First prize went to Mr Pye's bowl of roses.

"Finally," said the judge, "the prize for the most original display. This year we felt one entry beautifully captured our theme of 'Wild Nature'."

The judge held up a pot. It was Bertie's pot. "The winner," he said, "is Mrs Burns."

"That's us!" shouted Bertie, excitedly. Whiffer barked and strained on his lead, trying to reach his bone.

Mum looked at Bertie and then in

horror at the scruffy pot of weeds the judge was holding. "Bertie, that is *not* my flower arrangement," she hissed.

"No," admitted Bertie. "I had to make a few um … changes."

"Go on," Dad whispered to Mum. "They're all waiting."

Mum stepped forward to collect her prize, her face a deep shade of pink.

"Tell me," said the judge. "I'm curious. What gave you the idea of using a bone? Most original."

Mum shot a dark look at Bertie. "Oh it was my son's idea really. He can make a dog's dinner of anything."

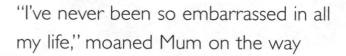

"I've never been so embarrassed in all my life," moaned Mum on the way home. "Mrs Nicely looked as if she was going to explode."

Bertie couldn't see what she was complaining about. After all, she wanted to win a prize and she had. You would have thought she'd be grateful! In any case things had worked out pretty well. His mum had won a gardening kit, which included a large pair of green gardening gloves. Bertie was wearing them now. They were the perfect thing for a bin man.